# *Dear Parent:*
## *Your child's love of reading starts here!*

Every child learns to read in a different way and at his or her own speed. Some go back and forth between reading levels and read favorite books again and again. Others read through each level in order. You can help your young reader improve and become more confident by encouraging his or her own interests and abilities. From books your child reads with you to the first books he or she reads alone, there are I Can Read Books for every stage of reading:

### SHARED READING
Basic language, word repetition, and whimsical illustrations, ideal for sharing with your emergent reader

### BEGINNING READING
Short sentences, familiar words, and simple concepts for children eager to read on their own

### READING WITH HELP
Engaging stories, longer sentences, and language play for developing readers

### READING ALONE
Complex plots, challenging vocabulary, and high-interest topics for the independent reader

I Can Read Books have introduced children to the joy of reading since 1957. Featuring award-winning authors and illustrators and a fabulous cast of beloved characters, I Can Read Books set the standard for beginning readers.

A lifetime of discovery begins with the magical words "I Can Read!"

*Visit www.icanread.com for information*
*on enriching your child's reading experience.*

I Can Read® and I Can Read Book® are trademarks of HarperCollins Publishers.

The Berenstain Bears: Too Much Noise!
Copyright © 2021 by Berenstain Publishing, Inc.
All rights reserved. Printed in the United States of America.
No part of this book may be used or reproduced in any manner whatsoever without written permission except
in the case of brief quotations embodied in critical articles and reviews. For information address HarperCollins
Children's Books, a division of HarperCollins Publishers, 195 Broadway, New York, NY 10007.
www.icanread.com

Library of Congress Control Number: 2021936539
ISBN 978-0-06-302444-1 (trade bdg.) — ISBN 978-0-06-302443-4 (pbk.)

Book design by Chrisila Maida

21 22 23 24 25   LSCC   10 9 8 7 6 5 4 3 2 1   ❖   First Edition

# The Berenstain Bears®
# Too Much NOISE!

## Mike Berenstain

Based on the characters created by
Stan and Jan Berenstain

**HARPER**
*An Imprint of HarperCollinsPublishers*

All is quiet in the Bear
family's tree house.
Mama and Papa are having
a quiet cup of tea.

"Ah! It's so quiet!" says Papa.

"Yes," says Mama, "so nice and quiet."

"Mama! Papa!" yell the cubs.

"Uh-oh!" says Papa.

"The cubs are awake."

Mama and Papa gulp their tea.

"Mama! Papa!" yell the cubs.

"Can we have breakfast?"

Mama and Papa help
the cubs get breakfast.
"Mama!" yells Sister.
"Brother's bumping me!"

"Papa!" yells Brother.

"Sister's shoving me!"

"Mama! Papa!" yells Honey,

just to join in.

Breakfast is over.

The cubs go into the family room.

They turn on the TV.

"BLAH! BLAH! BLAH!" goes the TV.

"BLAH! BLAH!"

Sister decides to put on some music.

"BOOM! BOOM! BOOM!"

goes the music.

"BOOM! BOOM!"

Brother starts playing a video game.

"BEEP! BEEP! BEEP!"

goes the video game.

"BEEP! BEEP!"

Sister wants to make a phone call.

"HELLO?" she yells over

the other noise.

"HELLO? HELLO? HELLO?"

Honey loves to play with

her Bearmo doll.

She pushes a button on the doll's back.

"HEE! HEE! HEE!" goes the doll.

"HEE! HEE!"

Brother thinks it's time
to practice his drums.

"POW! POW! POW!" go the drums.

"POW! POW!"

"QUIET!" yells Papa.

"QUIET!" yells Mama.

"QUIET! QUIET! QUIET!"

yell Mama and Papa.

"My goodness!" says Sister.
"Must you two really make
so much noise?"

"But . . ." says Papa.
"I'm surprised at you!"
says Brother.

"But . . ." says Mama.
"Hmph!" says Honey.

24

"We just wanted a little quiet," says Papa.

"Yes," says Mama, "just a little peace and quiet."

"Well, you don't have to yell,"
says Sister.

"Yes," says Brother, "you could
ask quietly."

"Yes!" says Honey.

Mama and Papa quietly
ask for a little quiet.
The cubs agree.

"Things are too noisy around here,"
says Brother.
"It would be nice to have
a little quiet for a change,"
says Sister.
"Nice!" says Honey.

The whole family spends some quiet time together.

Honey plays quietly.

Brother and Sister read quietly.

Mama sews quietly.

Papa takes a nap.

The only noise is Papa

softly snoring.

"Ah!" says the whole family.

"It's so quiet."